POPULAR HORSE BREEDS

MINIATURE HORSE

Marylou Morano Kjelle

EZ READERS

Creating Young Nonfiction Readers

EZ Readers lets children delve into nonfiction at beginning reading levels. Young readers are introduced to new concepts, facts, ideas, and vocabulary.

Tips for Reading Nonfiction with Beginning Readers

Talk about Nonfiction
Begin by explaining that nonfiction books give us information that is true. The book will be organized around a specific topic or idea, and we may learn new facts through reading.

Look at the Parts
Most nonfiction books have helpful features. Our *EZ Readers* include a Contents page, an Index, and color photographs. Share the purpose of these features with your reader.

Contents
Located at the front of a book, the Contents displays a list of the big ideas within the book and where to find them.

Index
An Index is an alphabetical list of topics and the page numbers where they are found.

Photos/Charts
A lot of information can be found by "reading" the charts and photos found within nonfiction text. Help your reader learn more about the different ways information can be displayed.

With a little help and guidance about reading nonfiction, you can feel good about introducing a young reader to the world of *EZ Readers* nonfiction books.

Mitchell Lane
PUBLISHERS

2001 SW 31st Avenue
Hallandale, FL 33009
www.mitchelllane.com

First Edition, 2021.

Author: Marylou Morano Kjelle
Designer: Ed Morgan
Editor: Morgan Brody

Names/credits:
Title: Miniature Horse / by Marylou Morano Kjelle
Description: Hallandale, FL :
Mitchell Lane Publishers, [2021]

Series: Popular Horse Breeds
Library bound ISBN: 978-1-68020-567-1
eBook ISBN: 978-1-68020-568-8

EZ readers is an imprint of Mitchell Lane Publishers.

Photo credits: Freepik.com, Shutterstock

CONTENTS

Words in **bold** can be found in the Glossary.

Miniature Horses are little horses. They are shorter than 34 inches (86 cm). They look like ponies, but they are adult horses.

Their **coats** are long and messy. They are many colors. Some Miniature Horses have spotted coats. Miniature Horses have thick **manes**. Their tails are thick too.

DID YOU KNOW?

The **pedigree** of Miniature Horses includes breeds from all over the world.

Miniature Horses weigh between 150–250 pounds (68–90 kg). They eat grass, hay, oats, and corn. They eat 2–5 pounds (about 1–2 kg) of food every day.

A baby horse is called a foal. It takes about 330 days (11 months) for a Miniature Horse foal to be born.

Miniature Horses live about 30 years.

DID YOU KNOW?

Some Miniature Horses have lived to be 35 years old.

Only small children should ride Miniature Horses.

Miniature Horses are good show horses. They pull small carts and wagons.

Did You Know?

They can pull loads that are **equal** to their own weight.

Some families keep Miniature Horses as pets.

DID YOU KNOW?

Miniature Horses make good guide horses. Like **seeing-eye dogs**, guide horses help people who have difficulty seeing.

Miniature Horses live in the United States. They are also found in other countries.

GLOSSARY

coat
The hair covering the body of an animal

equal
The same as

mane
Long hair on an animal's neck

pedigree
The family history of an animal

seeing-eye dog
A dog trained to guide a person who has difficulty seeing or is blind

Sources

Dutson, Judith. *96 Horse Breeds of North America*. North Adams, MA: Storey Publishers, 2005.

Edwards, Elwyn Hartley. *Horses*. London: Dorling Kindersley, 1993.

_____________ *Ultimate Horse*. London: Dorling Kindersley, 2002.

"Fast Facts." *Hendrick's Around the World in One Display*. http://www.hedricks.com/Promotions/aroundtheworldinonedisplay/Miniature-horse.html.

Harris, Moira C. *America's Horses: A Celebration of the Horse Breeds Born in the USA*. Guilford, CT: Lyons Press, 2003.

The History of the American Miniature Horse." *The Miniature Horse.com*. https://www.theMiniaturehorse.com/historyMiniatures.htm

"How much weight can a Mini Horse pull?" *Lil Beginnings Miniature Horses*. http://www.lilbeginnings.com/Miniature-horse-facts-and-information/how-much-weight-can-a-mini-horse-pull.shtml

Miniature Horse Facts." *Scott Creek.com*. https://www.scottcreek.com/mini-horse-facts.html

Further Reading

Web Pages

American Miniature Horse Association
www.amha.org

Blocksdorf, Katherine. "Fifteen Fascinating Facts About Horses"
https://www.thesprucepets.com/facts-about-horses-1887392

Miniature Horses as Pets
https://vetmed.tamu.edu/news/pet-talk/Miniature-horses-as-pets/

Books

Hansen, Grace. *Miniature Horses*. Mankato: Abdo Kids, 2016.

Matzke, Ann. *Mini Horse* (You Have a Pet What?!) Vero Beach: Rourke Educational Publishing, 2015.

Naviaux, Barbara. *Miniature Horses: Their Care, Breeding and Coat Colors*. Oxford: Raintree Publications, 1999.

Index

About the Author

Marylou Morano Kjelle lives and writes in Central New Jersey. She is a retired college English professor and the author of over 50 books on various topics for children and young adults. She learned a lot about the Miniature Horse while researching and writing this book. She thinks it's awesome that some Miniature Horses are trained to be guide pets and used to help people who are blind or have trouble seeing.